Georgie and the Dragon

Julia Jarman
and Damon Burnard

Collins

Best Friends • Jessy and the Bridesmaid's Dress •
Jessy Runs Away • **Rachel Anderson**
Changing Charlie • Clogpots in Space • **Scoular Anderson**
Ernest the Heroic Lion-tamer • Ivana the Inventor • **Damon Burnard**
Two Hoots • **Helen Cresswell**
Magic Mash • Nina's Machines • **Peter Firmin**
Shadows on the Barn • **Sarah Garland**
Clever Trevor • The Mystery of Lydia Dustbin's Diamonds • Nora Bone •
Nora Bone and the Tooth Fairy • **Brough Girling**
Sharon and Darren • **Nigel Gray**
Thing-in-a-Box • Thing-on-two-legs • **Diana Hendry**
Desperate for a Dog • More Dog Trouble • **Rose Impey**
Georgie and the Dragon • Georgie and the Planet Raider • **Julia Jarman**
Cowardy Cowardy Cutlass • Cutlass Rules the Waves • Free With Every Pack •
Mo and the Mummy Case • The Fizziness Business • **Robin Kingsland**
And Pigs Might Fly! • Albertine, Goose Queen • Jigger's Day Off
• Martians at Mudpuddle Farm • Mossop's Last Chance
• Mum's the Word • **Michael Morpurgo**
Granny Grimm's Gruesome Glasses • **Jenny Nimmo**
Grubble Trouble • **Hilda Offen**
Hiccup Harry • Harry Moves House • Harry's Party • Harry the Superhero •
Harry with Spots On • **Chris Powling**
Grandad's Concrete Garden • **Shoo Rayner**
Rattle and Hum – Robot Detectives • **Frank Rodgers**
Our Toilet's Haunted • **John Talbot**
Pesters of the West • **Lisa Taylor**
Lost Property • **Pat Thomson**
Monty the Dog Who Wears Glasses • Monty Bites Back • Monty Ahoy!
• Monty Must Be Magic! • Monty – Up To His Neck in Trouble! • **Colin West**
Ging Gang Goolie, It's an Alien • **Bob Wilson**

First published in Great Britain by
A & C Black (Publishers) Ltd 1991
First published by Collins 1992
20 19 18 17 16 15 14 13 12

Collins is an imprint of HarperCollins Children's Books part of
HarperCollins Publishers Ltd. 77-85 Fulham Palace Road, London W6 8JB

Text copyright © 1991 Julia Jarman
Illustrations copyright © 1991 Damon Burnard. All rights reserved.

ISBN 0-00-674137 1

Printed and bound in Great Britain by

Clays Ltd, St Ives plc

Chapter One

Georgie was a dragon killer. Saint George wasn't a patch on Georgie.

Nor were the Knights of the Round Table. Georgie had killed more dragons than all of them put together – and she'd rescued more damsels.

Her score for killing dragons was 1,072,372 (one million, seventy-two thousand, three hundred and seventy two).

Georgie's scores

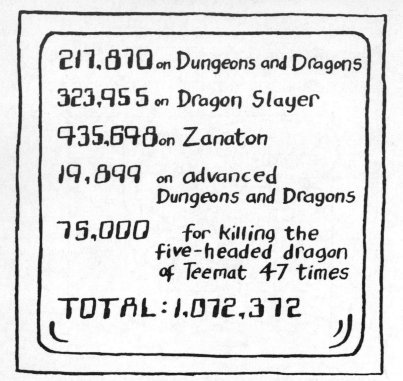

217,870 on Dungeons and Dragons

323,955 on Dragon Slayer

935,698 on Zanaton

19,899 on advanced Dungeons and Dragons

75,000 for killing the five-headed dragon of Teemat 47 times

TOTAL: 1,072,372

For Georgie, (as you'll have guessed, Super-Brain!) was a computer ace. And did she know it? Big Head wasn't the word. But she wasn't blood-thirsty. Her dragons were small and square and bouncy, so they didn't really get hurt. Or that's what she thought – until last Saturday . . .

That morning she was still in her pyjamas. The Tank was outside her bedroom door.

The Tank was Georgie's little sister. She was 2½ with golden curls and things shattered at her approach.

Silently Georgie
put another chair
against the door,
and some heavy books.
Then she switched
on her computer.

The screen shone green. So did her face. She could see it in the mirror – she loved that.

She slipped it into the disc drive.
Somehow she didn't notice the

The title appeared, then the instructions – in very tiny letters. She had to bend right up to the screen to read them.

Are you brave enough to face the vengeful dragon?

Press E to enter if the answer is YES.

Naturally Georgie pressed the E

and . . .

It didn't hurt or anything: the
screen sort of evaporated and there
she was flying through the air.

Meanwhile... Georgie?

The Tank was still
trying to get in
to Georgie's room.

Chapter Three

Then Georgie landed. She was leaning against a rock. Facing her was a dragon, reading a book.

'Ah,' said the dragon, 'I've been waiting for you.'

Georgie wasn't scared, of course. A dragon? So what? She'd zapped hundreds of them. This one looked old and slow.

But then he opened his jaws.
'Well now,' he said, 'best get it over with.'
'Get over what?' said Georgie.

But he didn't answer,
he just looked tetchy.

He said his teeth and his digestion
weren't what they used to be. Nor,
Georgie observed, were his legs.
And she'd just had a rather
disturbing thought.

So she ran, like a Force 9 gale,

under
his
sagging
belly

Chapter Four

The dragon didn't even try to chase
her – he just watched her run away.
But then she felt her bum burning.

Her pyjamas were on fire!

Georgie had to sit down suddenly to
put out the flames.
Then the dragon caught her.

You forgot
something about
dragons!

he said, sniggering
and blowing green
smoke rings.

He made her walk in front of him –
with her hands over the hole in her
pyjamas – and he started to talk
about recipes.

Georgie began to realise that she
was in a Very Tight Spot.
The dragon said that if he had to eat
her, she might as well taste good.
And he did have to – it was the Game.

That was it!
She would tell him a story so
edge-of-the-seat exciting that the
dragon would put off eating her
until he knew the ending.
But there wouldn't *be* an ending.
She would win!

NO!

roared
the dragon.

'SHUT YOUR MOUTH!
DON'T LIKE STORIES!
PIFFLE! WHIFFLE!
BALDERDASH!

So that was the end of that idea.
He liked facts, he said,
and only read
encyclopaedias.

She would have
to think of
something else.

Chapter Five

The dragon went off to some nearby woods for some charcoal, because he'd decided to barbecue her.

Suddenly . . .

it went dark.

In fact it went dark because the Tank, who was having a fine old time on Georgie's computer, had just turned the colour knob sharply to the left. Now she was pounding the keyboard as if it were a piano, singing at the top of her voice.

And, by chance, she pressed the Vertical Hold, very hard –

which made
Georgie vibrate –

which made
the ropes
come loose –

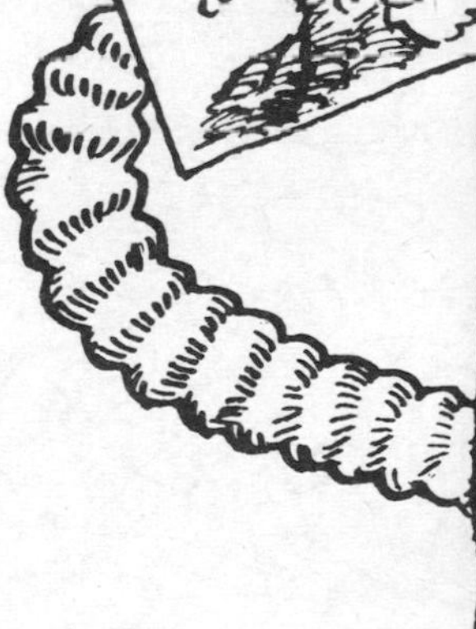

and the ground
beneath her
gave way!

THEN...

BASH!

The Tank hit the Shift key, which activated the Teleportation Slab beneath Georgie's feet.

Oo-er!

First she felt as if she was exploding

Then she felt herself re-forming –
and there she was . . .

standing in front of a king.

Georgie was wrong again.

Chapter Six

King Bert wasn't the protecting type. He was tall and droopy.

he said, and burst into tears.

Queen Ingrid, who was fat, was more perky. She told Georgie to make herself at home, which Georgie did.

She swam in
the royal bath.

She put on snazzy
new clothes.

Everybody was nice to her.
Especially Princess Elsie. The
princess looked a bit like the Tank.

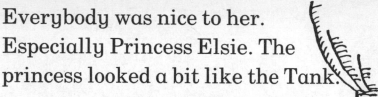

She said she was the king and
queen's only surviving daughter.
Her eight sisters had been eaten
by a dragon.

In the evening there was a royal
banquet. Georgie was the guest of
honour.

The queen announced that Georgie must eat heartily before *his* ordeal.

I'm not a his, I'm a her... and anyway, what's an ordeal?

But Queen Ingrid didn't seem to
hear. Now she was saying that Georgie
could have Princess Elsie's hand.

Her hand?
No thanks...

Everybody laughed.
It really was fun.
No one complained that she ate too much. No one mentioned bedtime. It was great. People seemed to think she was a boy, but what did that matter?

I didn't think it was funny...

That night she bounced fourteen times on the four-poster bed, then fell asleep.

Chapter Seven

Georgie
looked out
of the window.

There was the dragon, *her* dragon.

All that was left of the wood
was some ashes. He must have
thought she was hiding in it.

3 | Then they locked it behind her.

SLAM!

CLICK!

4 | She stood on the drawbridge — face to face with the dragon.

Chapter Eight

He was slabbering. There was slabber hanging from his mouth and a pool of slabber at his feet. You could see he was expecting a nice juicy princess. And when he saw a knight in armour, he was not pleased.

The dragon spat scornfully.

He charged – snorting smoke and flames.

Then he swooped.

Clawed.

Ripped.

Munched.

Gulped.

It was over very quickly.

Chapter Nine

Georgie felt quite sick, watching it.
For, thanks to the Tank, she had
escaped once again!

Seconds before the drawbridge was
raised, the Tank had hit the pause
button . . .

For a few moments, everyone
froze, except Georgie.

Quickly she climbed out of the
armour and stuffed it with smelly
socks.

(They belonged to the
gatehouse keeper.)

Then she heaved the pongy
armour onto an ancient
skateboard and sent it forth
into battle – where the dragon
had eaten the lot! Now he
had terrible indigestion.

The noise was terrible. Everyone at court was weeping and wailing, too – for Georgie and for the little princess.

'Oh no you won't,' thought Georgie, 'because I have a plan.'

Chapter Ten

A few minutes later, she was rising from the heap of chewed up armour, wearing the gate-keeper's night-shirt.

The dragon
looked up –
and fainted.

'Great so far,' thought Georgie.
She glided towards him. The
dragon opened one eye.

So she haunted him all the way
back to his lair,

where, once the door was locked, he
started to make suspicious remarks.
Like 'Oh ghostie, what solid arms
you've got.'
She kept them well hidden.
And 'Oh ghostie, what a high girlie
voice you've got.'
She made it low and spooky.

The dragon gave her a hard stare.
Georgie stared defiantly back.

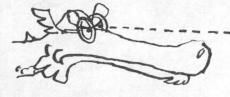

The dragon seemed to give in. He looked away. Then turned . . . and grabbed Georgie!

You're Georgie Bell, aren't you? The REAL THING. Not a ghost at all. You don't fool me!

oo-er!

He accused her of killing all
his relations: his granny, his aunty,
his uncle Bill, his cousin Dwayne
and his wife Hilda.

He was the only surviving dragon,
he said, and he had been waiting for
this moment. Now it was time for

THE DRAGON'S REVENGE!

48

The dragon was thoughtful.

Georgie explained that he had to mix wine and oil and herbs. And she would have to lie down in it.

And so . . .

The marinade was quite a good idea
because it gave her time. But it was
yukky lying in it.
'How long?' said the dragon.
'All night is best,' said Georgie,
who was hoping she could escape
in the dark.

Chapter Eleven

But the dragon kept coming back to roll Georgie over. He said knees and elbows were the toughest bits. He was getting hungry, and he didn't know if he could wait until morning.

Why don't you have boiled eggs tonight—they're quite easily digested!

He found some eggs at the back of the cave, then went off to get some water.

Georgie hunched up in the sticky grunge. She could hear a squeaking and a tap-tapping. They seemed to come from the eggs.

The dragon came back and put the water on to boil. Georgie didn't mention the noises. She suggested he made some toast soldiers to go with the eggs. The dragon pottered off.

Georgie investigated further

She grabbed a spoon. A few seconds later, she was balancing the half-hatched eggs over the boiling water.

The dragon looked.

The dragon was desperate.

I can, dragon. I've got to. That's the stupid game, isn't it? It's dragon kill Georgie, or Georgie kill the dragons. That's the rule. Look in the stupid rule book!

So was Georgie.

Get the rule book, dragon, and put a pencil in my hand!

Chapter Twelve

The dragon and Georgie both promised
to change their ways. The dragon
made lentil soup for tea. Then he
played with his children by the fire.

Georgie played too, for a bit. But watching them, she started to miss her family – even her horrible little sister. And by Amazing Coincidence, right at that moment, the Tank's pudgy finger landed on the Exit key of Georgie's computer.

And Georgie   EXITED!

VROOSH!

She was flying again!